American Ghost Stories

A collection by S. K. Dines

American Ghost Stories is a collection of fictional short stories written by Shana Dines.

Subtle horror unexpected is many times more chilling and terrifying than horror that smacks you in the face. Be prepared to be terrified. Horror in the dark or during a storm is expected. Terror when your guard is not up is sometimes even more terrifying. Who expects to be confronted with horror when the sun is shining? Sit back and relax and prepare to be entertained with the unexpected.

TABLE OF CONTENTS

Just Deserts

When he took his woman to be his lawfully wedded wife, he had no doubt that she was the woman of his dreams. His raven-haired beauty, with her porcelain skin, model's figure, and soft-spoken manner, was everything that Mommy was not.

The Cow! How he loathed his mother. The demanding, controlling, demeaning old bitch! He hoped he never set eyes on her again. Of course Gina loved his mother. She was the mother that she never had. Her mother on the other hand never gave a damn about her or spent any time with her so his mother was all that she needed to help her feel special.

You have to take the bitter with the sweet, Joe told himself. He guessed he would have to let well enough alone. Gina was easy to control and manipulate, and since after all he was handicapped, it was easier to get her to take care of him.

"Gin, do this! Gin do that!" and all he had to do was crack the whip from his wheelchair and he had her running to do his bidding. When she pouted once in a while… wanting to do something with her friends or to just watch something that she wanted to watch on television, well… it was easy enough to lay a guilt trip on her. "Look, Gin, I'd do it myself if I could. I hate to ask you to do things for me. You know that! It's just this damn chair! I can't do it," he pathetically wailed. Once in a while, he got a nagging feeling, kinda like someone blowing cold air on the back of his neck. Or he could feel the hair on his head, even on the back of arms, stand up. It was eerie. He couldn't explain it. It actually sounded stupid to voice it. There was just something vaguely uncomfortable, creepy going on. Maybe it was a certain look she gave him or a turn of the head. Her head didn't spin around or anything, like Linda Blair in the movie, it was just a certain, tilt, or turn, whatever. He knew it was ridiculous, but it was there. Even when they were dating, he really intentionally looked for someone, NOT like his mother!

Gina was so quiet. She was shy and she had this way of almost shuffling, crab like, oh yeah, I know it doesn't sound very appealing, but it wasn't as unappealing as it sounds. Maybe he should say more Geisha girlish. She talked in quiet, hushed whispers, in a little girl's voice. He actually found it to be quite the turn-on. He needed control. He loved control, and this was one girl he could control. She was always apologizing. If the sun didn't shine, she apologized."Oh Joooeee. I'm sorry the sun isn't shining. I'm soorry, the soup's too hot. I'm soorrry, it's Monday. I'm soooorrrry your butt is sore." Actually it got a bit nauseating sometimes. "For Christ's sake Gin, quit being sorry for every fuckin thing! Then she would cringe, and say "I'm sorry." This of course made him fume in rage and in frustration. But all in all…he loved having control of her.

The hardest thing for him was to let her work. He didn't want her out of his sight. What if she found another guy, one who for instance could walk? One who treated her well, one who she would fawn over instead of him? Then what? But he loved money, and he sure wasn't making it on disability. So he decided as long as she was so attached to his Mommy, maybe she could work where his Mother worked. Mommy would make sure there was no hanky-panky going on.

When Mommy came to pick up Gina to take her to work, God knows he couldn't let her go by herself, he would watch them leave through the picture window, already wishing that she were there to stick his dinner in the microwave for him. That is, the dinners that she prepared ahead of time. He didn't like any of that store bought frozen "shit." It wasn't like he couldn't do it. He preferred not to. That's what a wife is for. But then again you have to "Take the bitter with the sweet." Right? The hackles on the back of his neck would rise as Mommy and Gina simultaneously lifted their hands up to wave good-bye to him. What was it? What was it that made his blood run cold as he watched them drive away?

One of the things that he loved about Gina was her hair, the only drawback being its color. She had beautiful raven black hair, thick, curly, mass oftumbling soft fragrant waves. He loved to press his face into it, when he held her, when they made love, when they slept spoon style. Yeah, it was the same color and texture of his mother's, but hers was short and stubby now.

He also loved her skin. She was one of those raven haired Irish beauties, with skin as fair as milk, a light dusting of freckles, coloring her cheeks, her throat. Okay, so she had the same coloring as his mother, but Gina was delicate, actually others had called her anorexic. She didn't eat for days, which kept her reed thin, not like his mother, the cow, who had billows and pillows of fat around her neck, belly and …. He couldn't believe that those two little chicken legs could hold up that tomato body. Not his Gina! She was beautiful, tall, willowy and all his. His every wish was her command. He had to keep her in line. That was the only problem. He had to be on his toes every minute, which for him of course was a bit of a problem. He still used those damn literal phrases of course he meant that he had to keep an eye on her all the time. So, as soon as she walked in the door from work, usually after 10 hours, he wanted supper started. She was "the little woman" after all. That was the one good thing he learned from his son-of-a-bitch father. "By God, you gotta let'em know who's boss!" Joe was no doubt "the boss."

"Joe, pronounced *Jooooe.* I'm tired; can't we go out to eat tonight?" She whined, scrunching her face up, her eyes almost disappearing. It was almost like oh… there was that feeling again.

"What? I'm not made out of money you know!" He barked at her.

"But *Jooooe!* I'm tirrrrred!" She would scrunch again.

"You just get in there and rattle those pots and pans, Woman!" This was another fine line he learned from Daddy Dearest. "Why can't we ever just go out and eat?" she persisted, so unlike her. So he would have to wheel up and give her a friendly little smack upside the head. Fortunately for her she could run a little faster than he could wheel, which would just piss him off. So he would make her stand there so he could give her a little slug. She would slouch down and cry big crocodile tears. He really didn't hit her *THAT* hard. She'd shuffle out of the room snuffling back her snot and tears to begin preparing dinner. He would majestically roll back out to the television watching a porno flick.

Sitting at the table eating, in her case very little, usually after eating she would disappear and he would hear her puking up good food that he paid for. Well, maybe he didn't pay for it, but anyway, you get the picture. Soon his mother came in, without knocking as usual. She pulled up a chair next to Gina, after grabbing herself a plate, loading it full of spaghetti, and then started shoveling it into her mouth. She complimented Gina on her culinary skills. When his mother looked over at Gina, Joe felt his blood run cold. Oh God, what is it? There was something, something… he couldn't put his finger on it. He thought he was gonna lose his cookies. His mother and Gina, both of them together, what a fine pair they would make with separate bathrooms to vomit in! Jesus! He couldn't tell what it was, but he felt rank horror, looking from one of them to the other. That night in bed, he pulled the covers over his head, just like he used to when his mother came in to tuck him in at night, smothering him with her massive breasts against him.

He stayed firmly on his side of the bed. He didn't even spoon Gin and nestle his nose into her fragrant long hair. Then it hit him! Jesus! That was it! She cut her fuckin hair! He hadn't even noticed. She cut her fuckin hair! It was exactly like his mother's! She didn't even ask him!

When she came home from work a couple a nights later, he was in the driveway waiting for her. Jack, his poker buddy was just leaving. They'd had a few brewskies, played a few hands of poker, and Joe lost a couple hundred bucks. Oh well, Gin could work more overtime. No big deal.

Jack looked up at Joe, puzzled. "Hey! Gin sure looks like her mom, can't hardly tell the difference. I wouldn't mind banging her! I mean her mother, not your wife! Well, her too, *hhhhaaaaaa,* just teasing! They are quite the babes." Believe me, neither one of them were babes by any stretch of the imagination, not anymore anyway. It hit Joe like a ton of bricks.

"Jack,you idiot! That's not Gin's mother! That's my mother!" "Well, hot damn, Joe, you got an old lady just like the one who married dear old dad!" Jack snorted and guffawed his way out to his pick-up.

Gin poured out of the car, and his mother waved and backed out. He shuddered in revulsion, rolling into the house, not even demanding dinner before he said hi.

They ate in silence as denial washed over him in waves. This can't be. This is my wife. She ain't a thing like the old lady. He asked her why she cut her hair, and she replied that it was easier to take care of. He watched her shovel food in her mouth, then get up from the table, burping, and

wiping her mouth on the back of her hand. Jesus! No! It can't be he thought. Where was he when she started piling on the pounds?

He went to bed early that night. He lay in bed and shuddered, incredulous, "I must be fuckin crazy," he thought quietly. He dozed, nightmares invading his sleep. The moon poured in gently.

In his sleep he felt the bed give way. He awoke with a start. He saw Gin leaning over him. The moonlight backlit her face as it loomed over him, her pendulous breasts squashing him. It was his mother's face. His mother's body as she pressed into him. She turned her face toward him.

Her face was his mother's! *"Holy Mother of God!"* Ya reap what ya sow, and ya gotta take the bitter with the sweet!" He married his mother after all! *"Just Deserts!"*

The Haunted Clown Doll

I wanted to get something special for my little girl and time was running out. I was coming home after the weekend, after going to Aunt Carrie's funeral. She had been ill but no one expected her to die so suddenly. I went to be with my family, and since Katie didn't know most of the relatives, I left her home with her father. Jake hadn't got to spend much time bonding with her and he didn't really know my Aunt Carrie. We hadn't been married that long and we hadn't been back to Vermont since we had gotten married. I hate to admit it was just too much hassle. I had a very difficult pregnancy and my doctor advised me not to travel. We didn't expect to start a family so soon, so things just moved too fast, and we moved to slow. Now I was sorry we hadn't gone back to visit and it was too late.

I already stopped at a book store and got Jake a book by one of his favorite authors, so now I needed to get something for Katie. She would soon be four and she loved dolls especially clown dolls. I don't know why. I sure didn't! When I saw the little antique store with the little clown doll in the window, I knew that was what I wanted to get for her. Leaving the store I couldn't help thinking, what on earth possessed me to buy this? It was cute enough, as far as clowns go. But I figured that just because I didn't like clowns, there was no need to deprive my daughter.

I thought, "Okay, I will bond with this thing." So, on a whim I propped it up. I mean her. I propped her up on the front seat in the passenger seat and put the seat belt on her. "Well, I guess you and I may as well learn to be friends for Katie's sake," I said to her. She sat mutely and unappreciatively next to me. I have to admit she was an easy passenger. No talking back, no passenger side driving. I laughed snidely to myself. She sat smugly staring out the front window. Okay, she was a little short, but if she looked up, she could look out the window. I said to myself again. She had a mop of red hair, and looked similar to Raggedy Annie, although she had a white face. Her eyes were the kind that closed and shut. They were black. She had the traditional little apron and striped leggings on. I was thinking to myself, "Why didn't I just buy her a little baby doll? *A NEW one!*" This thing was an antique, and there was something creepy about it. I felt bad about thinking that. It isn't Katie's fault that I don't like clowns. I didn't want to put my fears on her. Just because I had been terrified by a neighborhood clown when I was little that didn't mean that she should be afraid!I cranked the radio up and listened to some good old rock and roll, singing to the music. I stopped at a red light and turned to see if the road was clear, and when I turned back around, I would have sworn that the doll had turned her head. I felt my skin prickle.

I looked at her and jokingly said, "Did you see something?"

I would have named her, but since she was to be Katie's doll, I didn't think that was fair. But I found myself calling her Maude! How is that for a lovely name? Then I thought, "Eewww! That is the name of the old lady clown in the neighborhood that scared the bejesus out of me." It was unconscious I was sure, but it still didn't settle my nerves any.

I pulled into the driveway, feeling a rush of joy and relief. I was excited to be with my little family again. Jake ran out and scooped me up in his arms, no easy feat, and kissed me soundly on the lips. After Jake put me down, little Katie threw her arms around my legs. I picked her up and held her close to me, breathing in her fresh little four-year-old smell. They must have anticipated my early arrival, and she was all bathed and freshly dressed. Her little curls glistened in the sunlight.

Look at what I got for you Precious! I proudly picked up the doll and deposited it in her arms. She kissed her and pronounced her Maude! I felt horror wash over me. I didn't call the doll Maude to her.

"Why do you want to call her Maude?" I asked her.

"I don't know Mama, she just looks like a Maude to me," she said with childlike dignity.

"Do you know anyone by that name, Honey," I asked her casually.

"No Mama, I just think she looks like a Maude," she seriously answered.

I looked over her head at Jake, and made a face, and he laughed, and made one back at me.

"Oh Honey that is a perfectly nice name!" Jake said with much gusto. Just then the Pizza guy drove up with my favorite pizza. Antonio's.

"Oh Jake, thank you so much, I am so tired, the last thing I wanted to think about was having to make dinner." I gushed thankfully.

"Anything for you sweetheart. I know this weekend must have been hard for you. I am sorry we didn't go with you." He smiled.

After getting the dinner out of the way, and putting Katie to bed with Maude, blah. We cuddled up in front of the fireplace, a glass of white wine for me and a beer for Jake. I told him about the funeral and how I wanted to go back at least once a year to spend more time with my mother. I realized more and more how short life is. Jake agreed and we even talked about going there for a beautiful Vermont Christmas. We made out as in days of old, and talked about how lucky we were to have our perfect little family.

I couldn't help but feel an ominous chill in the air. I couldn't put my finger on it, but when we went to bed, I found myself wishing I wouldn't have gotten that doll for Katie. *"Stupid, stupid, stupid,"* I thought to myself.

We always left the hall light on so if Katie woke up she wouldn't be afraid. But when we made love we would close the door, almost all the way, so we could hear her if she got up. We were in the middle of a rather heated, passionate love making session and I with eyes half closed could see over Jake's shoulder. Just as we were fully into it, I saw the door move. The hall light was glaring in my face. I thought it was Katie, and whispered to Jake.

He quickly jumped up and went to comfort Katie, but she wasn't there. The mood was interrupted and I went in to see if she had gotten back in bed, but she was sleeping soundly.

Maude was sitting in her little rocker across the room, with a mocking look on her face. I swear to it. I couldn't sleep the rest of the night, but told myself that I must be dreaming. Jake was not a very happy camper after having our time interrupted. He got up and went to work, a little surly and disappointed. Katie bounded down the stairs, Maude in hand. She plumped her little body into the chair at the table. I made her a kitty shaped pancake, and she chattered away about nursery school.

"Can I take Maude with me today?" She asked excitedly.

"Sure Honey, you can take her with you." I replied.

I hate to confess I was glad she wasn't going to be staying home with me, Maude that is.

"Why did you take Maude out of my bed last night Mama?" Katie innocently asked.

"Honey I thought you did?" I cautiously asked back.

"No Mama you did!" She sternly answered.

"Oh I am sorry I don't remember that." I slowly replied.

I didn't want to scare her, but I knew I hadn't taken that damn doll out of her bed. I knew that it wasn't Katie who opened our door either.

I dropped them off at the preschool and came home trying to reason with myself. What the hell was wrong with me? Was this some kind of morbid grieving thing going on? Was I grieving over Aunt Carrie? I knew I had an active imagination, but this was really creepy. I took a long leisurely bath and read a book in the bathtub. This is one of the most relaxing things that I like to do. The sun streamed through the window, and I watched the birds in the backyard. We have a large backyard and a privacy fence, so I feel secure doing that. I was beginning to doze, and I heard a giggle. Actually it was more like a cackle. I felt the hair rise up on the back of my neck. There was no one in the house but me. I cocked my head, and listened. I heard it again.

I froze. It stopped and I quietly got out of the tub, grabbing my terry cloth robe. I tip toed down to Katie's room and in horror looked into the face of Maude. She was again sitting in the little rocking chair. I know I saw her eyes blink. Slowly I saw the rocking chair move, and she was rocking and grinning, malevolently at me! I backed out of the bedroom, clutching my robe close to me. Maude continued rocking toward me and I continued backwards towards the top of the steps. I stepped backwards and felt myself lose balance. Oh, my God, who is going to get Katie from school! I felt myself falling down the stairs, and then I lost consciousness. The last thing I remember is that thing, backing me up to the stairs and it was laughing.

"Honey, oh my God!" I heard Jake calling me. I was in the hospital, and they ran every test known to man on me to see if I was okay. When I hadn't shown up for Katie her teacher called for me. When she was unable to get me she called Jake. That's when they knew something was wrong. I told Jake we had to get the clown doll out of the house! I told him it was evil.

"Okay sweetheart, you are going to be fine." He soothed.

I felt better knowing that he was taking care of it. I told him to burn it or take it to the landfill, anything, just get rid of it. It was evil. I told him what happened. Unfortunately he thought it was the head injury that was causing me to be delusional.

I saw Katie's sweet little face above me. "Oh sweetheart I am so sorry I wasn't there to pick you up! Were you scared?" I soothed.

"Yes Mama, I was scared and I couldn't find Maude! Why did you take her home? I wanted to show her to my friends for show and tell and she wasn't in her seat! Then you didn't come to get me and I was mad!" she pouted.

I hid my shock over her doll, and told her that I was sorry that I had fallen down. I didn't forget her. I had gotten hurt, but I was okay now. She seemed to be content with that. I told her that I would get her a new doll though, that Maude had an accident, and I was very sorry but she couldn't be repaired. I hoped that she would be satisfied with my answer. How that possessed doll came home, I didn't know, but she, or it, would be gone permanently! What the hell was I thinking? I must have been out of my mind to bring that monster home! I could still picture that hideous little grinning face, malevolently leering at me. I shuddered involuntarily.

I was so glad to get home, and again, we had my favorite pizza. I felt loved and cherished by my husband. He seemed to have a sense for what I needed; hot chocolate by the fireplace, and an icepack for my head, what a combination, but it worked for me. I called for Katie and waited for her to come and cuddle with me, fresh from her bath. I was still wobbly and my head still ached from the fall on the hard steps. Luckily it was only a mild concussion.

Katie plunked down beside me on the couch, and laid her little curly head on my lap. I looked in horror as she laid Maude next to her on my knee! I jerked unable to control my terror.

Katie innocently said, "Mama, look! Daddy found Maude. She was lying on your bed! I am so glad she is safe. I thought she was lost when you said that you didn't bring her home and that she had an accident! She is fine!"

I looked over at Jake, and he looked down sheepishly.

"I guess the Dr. was able to fix her up after all Honey."

The revulsion that I felt for that doll and for Jake and his betrayal was hard to hide. How could he do that? How could he not get rid of this thing? Katie giggled with delight over finding Maude, as she looked over Maude at her hero father. She didn't see what I saw. Maude's eyes rolled up at me and her mouth turned in an evil leering grin at me. I felt the air around me become frigid.

"Mama, it's cold over here! Poor Maude is cold too!" She got up and moved closer to the fireplace. I wanted to throw that horror into the fireplace. I couldn't believe that Jake didn't destroy it! I cannot begin to describe the revulsion, fear and loathing that I felt in my own house. I thought it was over and now it was back.

"How could you? How could you not get rid of that thing?" I spat under my breath in bed later that night. "I told you it caused me to fall down the stairs! It is evil! I know that it is hard to believe but I know it is evil! You promised me!" I began to cry, trying not to lose control. We were in bed, and I could not bear to think of that thing waiting, in my baby's room. Waiting for what? Oh God! What was going to happen? How could I leave my baby sleeping in her room with that monster? I would have to take it away from her and get rid of it when she was sleeping.

"Honey, you are over reacting, it is only a doll." Jake soothed.

"It is not only a doll! I tell you it is haunted!" I screamed.

I would have gotten rid of it, but I thought you were just affected by the fall. I am sorry for your sake that I didn't, but Katie loves that doll, and Honey I am sorry but I can't believe that a doll is haunted." He shook his head in disbelief. "I would have gotten rid of it; if I would have known it would upset you this much, but Honey I just don't believe that it is possible. I am sorry, I just can't."

I was fuming with indignation! "How can you not believe me? Even if you didn't believe me, why couldn't you do what I asked?"

"Well Katie loved that doll so much, I just couldn't justify it," Jake humbly replied.

I made up my mind as soon as Katie was asleep; Maude's ass was in the fireplace! I lay there waiting for the soft snoring sounds of Jake. When I was sure he was asleep, I crept into Katie's room, and gently went to pry Maude from Katie's arms. She moaned softly in her sleep, Katie not Maude. Maude's hideous black eyes flew open in obvious rage. I recoiled in horror, but picked the vile thing up by her arm. I carried her out of Katie's room like it was a poisonous snake! Rushing out of her room, I hurried down the stairs as fast as I could and turned the gas fireplace on. When the flames shot up, I tossed the hissing vile thing in the flames. I swear she screamed in rage, and when she whooshed up in flames, I saw her writhe and toss in incensed madness! The smell was the most atrocious sulphurous stench of decomposed, rank abomination that one can imagine. It was like the odor of decaying burnt flesh.

I opened the front door, allowing the fresh air to wash out the acrid stench. The sense of relief I felt is indescribable. I went to bed, woodenly, and prayed, asking God to help us all. I tossed and turned all night, but was ready to face the wrath of my little Katie and Jake about the missing witch.

Nothing prepared me for what came in the morning. Katie bounded into bed with Jake and me ready for a day of cartoons and fun. She plopped her little sleep-warmed body between Jake and I and snuggled up next to us. I smiled in half sleep, throwing my arm over the two of them, and then I felt it, the cold rigid evil in Katie's arms. I opened my eyes in horror, and grinning into my face, were the malevolent eyes of Maude! I jumped up and out of bed, shuddering and quaking in revulsion! I couldn't scream or voice my shock, because Katie and Jake didn't know what I had done!

Oh my God, oh my God, oh my God, it just kept running through my head. *Oh my God,* what am I gonna do? The terror and confusion were indescribable.

"Come back to bed, sweetheart," Jake cajoled.

"I have to go to the bathroom," I replied.

"Oh come on it is Sunday morning, let's skip church and just lay around today," He coaxed.

"No, I want to make a big breakfast, and then you guys can come down when it is ready." I was buying time.

I hurried up, heart pounding and raced downstairs. I could still smell the awful odor in the living room. I felt nauseous. Was I losing my mind? How could Maude come back? I burned her, and I could still smell the hellish odor in the air. She was upstairs in bed with my husband and daughter. How was that possible? My God how was that possible?

I started whipping up batter for waffles. At least I could keep my mind working, while I prepared breakfast. I really needed to talk to our priest. But I didn't know how to approach him. Would he think I was crazy too? The sun shone beautifully through the bay window, and I wanted so badly to believe that this was not real. Maybe this was like before. Maybe I was hallucinating? How else could you explain it?

Jake nuzzled my neck, and I jumped a mile. "God Jake, you scared the crap out of me! Don't sneak up on me like that!" I cried.

"Sorry Honey, you used to like that. What the hell is that rank smell? Something die in here? Jesus, it stinks!" He wrinkled his nose up.

"I burned Maude last night." I spat out.

"Ha ha, sure, that is why she is up in bed with Katie." Jake replied.

"I am serious, I burned her up, and that is the smell from her possessed, evil body!" I spat out woodenly.

Jake laughed nervously. "Come on Melissa, you can't be serious?"

"I am serious Jake. I don't know how she came back, but I burned her in the fireplace after you and Katie went to sleep. She was hissing, and spitting, and writhing, and pure evil. I tossed the little bitch in the fireplace and watched her burn in hell!" I cried.

"Melissa, I am sorry but I can't believe that. I am afraid that you need to see Dr. Matthews again. She was able to help you before, and I believe you need to see her again. I believe that you believe this, but Honey it can't be true. I haven't witnessed anything, and neither has Katie, and she loves that doll. Frankly I am surprised that you bought that doll, the way you hate clowns?"Why? After what happened to you? Why would you buy a clown doll for Katie?" Jake shook his head worriedly.

"I don't know Jake, I really don't know. The instant I put her in the car, I felt like I was making a mistake. But it was like I was compelled to do it. Maybe I should see Dr. Matthews. Would you call her for an emergency appointment for me tomorrow? I want to get rid of this thing as soon as possible. Either I am crazy or that thing is possessed," I whispered.

Katie came bounding down the stairs, Maude in tow. She plopped in her chair, and put Maude in the chair next to her. I shuddered and stole a glance at Maude. She looked like she always did, just like a stuffed harmless doll. I must be losing it. I was determined to solve this tomorrow.

The rest of the day was uneventful, as far as Maude goes. We went to the park and ate at

McDonald's. Katie and Maude played in the outdoor playground, and I was hoping Katie would forget her, or some little heathen would stomp her to death on the playground. No such luck. The hideous thing sat in the back seat with Katie on the way home. She was mute, and grotesque, but at least she was not alive, or should I say she wasn't real.

Putting Katie to bed that night was terrifying. How could I let that thing sleep with her? How could I leave her unprotected? I took out my crucifix, and slipped it over Katie's head, before I went to bed. At least I felt a little better about leaving her in there with Maude.

When we were in bed Jake told me I had an appointment with Dr. Matthews in the morning at 10:00. I felt a wave of fear and relief at the same time. Dr. Matthews could help me one way or another. She did before and I believed she could again. She wouldn't pull any punches with me either. I slept fitfully, but was relieved in the morning to see that Katie was okay and Maude was still her old dumb self.

"Mama, why is that cross laying on the floor?" Katie asked me innocently.

"What do you mean on the floor honey?" I asked quietly.

"When I got up and put my dirty clothes in the clothes hamper, your cross was on the floor, under my dirty clothes." Katie explained quizzically.

What the hell was she talking about? If I told her I put it on her in the night, she would question that. I didn't know what to say, except I was horrified at the thought that somehow that crucifix was removed from my daughter during the night. I didn't do it, and she probably didn't do it, so what happened? Jake had already left for work and I doubted that he did it, but then I didn't know for sure. Maybe he was afraid that Katie would get twisted in it somehow. Well it was too late to ask him and one way or another that bitch Maude was going to die! I would see Dr. Matthews and she would have to help me, that was all there was to it. She had to help me or I would lose my mind, or my daughter.

Katie skipped out to the car with Maude by the arm. She carefully buckled her in a seat belt, and I helped her into her booster seat. I avoided Maude." Come on, this is ridiculous!" I thought. But I felt the hair on the back of my neck prickle. When I dropped them off at the door and waved goodbye to Katie and Mrs. Wilson, I breathed a sigh of relief. Now how in the hell would I explain this to Dr. Matthews? I appreciated it that Dr. Matthews would always meet me at the door. She stood about five-foot, but was very confident, warm and friendly. She had honey blonde hair, which she wore in a classic page boy style. She had a lightweight sage green sweater that complimented her beautiful dark fringed hazel eyes. She was small but built perfectly. I always felt rather dowdy around her. She was very professional, but within minutes of being with her I felt comfortable and cared for.

She always showed remarkable concern, warmth and kindness. I always felt funny calling her by her first name, but she always reminded me that she preferred to have me call her Amanda. She was like an older sister. She probably was old enough to be my mother, but didn't look a day over forty.

Head down, I told her the story. I was afraid to look up, but when I finished, I looked up out of the corner of my eye. I had to see her reaction. Would she think I was crazy? Would she tell me it was my imagination or what? I wasn't prepared for her expression. I know that she would work hard at remaining neutral, even when some of the experiences I shared with her were pretty horrific but nothing prepared me for her response.

Her large expressive eyes registered horror and shock. "Oh my Melissa, I don't know quite what to say. This is really quite a shocking thing to deal with. I know that you are not delusional. I know that you have had experiences in the past, that if I didn't know your history, I would have a hard time accepting, but this is something I will have to absorb a little slowly. I do believe in the possibility of supernatural occurrences. I have not experienced any myself, but I don't discredit others' experiences. Melissa, the shocking thing is that you would buy a clown doll, considering your past experience. Would you like to explain why you would do that?"

"I don't know Amanda. I can't explain it. It was like a compulsion. Maybe I was trying to work out the past? At first I didn't even think of it. I just wanted to get something for Katie that she likes. I don't want to put my fears onto her. But once I got that thing in the car, I didn't know what to do. So I just tried to pooh pooh it. But when Katie said that her name was Maude, it was like I had been hit in the stomach with a bowling ball," I said.

"Oh Melissa, I believe that you believe it. What does Jake say?" she cautiously asked.

"Ha ha, Jake sent me to see you to see what you thought," I sarcastically snorted. "I think he just wants you to fix me again like you did before."

"Melissa, I didn't "fix" you. I helped you to work through your past abuse. What you experienced was horrible. Don't make light of it. It is no wonder that you are having a hard time with this. I don't know what to make of it, but I believe that you believe it. I don't think that you are crazy. It has to be coincidence, or maybe Katie heard you mention that name and it just stuck, without her knowing how that name was associated with you. We will work this out though Melissa. I will help you. I never experienced anything to the degree that you did, but I don't think I would want a doll around that looks the way you described that one. I am concerned though that it is around you with the way you feel about it. It will be hard for you to explain to Katie though about her disappearance. I would not usually recommend this, but I think that you need to have Jake dispose of the doll, with you, without Katie of course. You will have to tell her something that will satisfy her. I am really perplexed about how to tell you to do this. But for your sake you need to see it disposed of with someone you trust. You need to know that it is gone. I think with the absolutely horrific abuse that you suffered by that evil woman, Maude, maybe it triggered some kind of abreaction. I know you are sane Melissa. You just need to know that, too.

Then maybe we need to have some more sessions to deal with the abuse. Maybe there is more that you need to process. You are doing so well and should be proud of your accomplishments. I don't want your past to come back to haunt you," Amanda worriedly explained.

She had Jake come in after work and told him what the plan was. He wasn't thrilled about the idea, but was willing to go along with it. We had to decide what to tell Katie. I called our friends, Bill and Sharon and asked if it was okay for Katie to spend the night with Kelly that I was still recovering from my fall and needed to see the Dr. early in the morning. Sharon said she would be glad to and that she could take both the girls to school in the morning.

Now we had to put our plan in action. I looked at Jake with terror in my eyes. Was this the right thing to do? We were lying to our daughter, but how could we tell her the truth? Even though Jake may not believe me, he was willing to do what Amanda suggested, but I could tell he had misgivings about it. Not me! I was ready to do anything to get rid of that evil thing. I still couldn't believe that I had hallucinated burning her. But what other possible explanation was there? Or should I say "rational" explanation?

We rushed Katie, getting her ready to go to the Martins' house, hoping that she would forget Maude. We packed her overnight bag together, and listened to her chatter about going to her little friend's house. I kept diverting her from Maude. I felt less guilt than hope that I could keep her distracted with conversation.

"No! I forgot Maude!" Katie wailed.

"Oh sweetheart I am sorry, we can't be late. Martin's are taking you to Pizza Hut. We can't go back, or it will be too late," I guiltily soothed. How could I ever forgive myself, and how would I explain Maude's absence? I would deal with that later. Katie was crying softly when we left her at the Martins. I felt bad but relieved that she didn't put up too much of a fuss. She was sidetracked by their cocker spaniel and Kelly, too. We made our arrangements, and said our good-byes.

Jake sullenly got in the driver's seat. I felt defensive and stupid. "Honey, I know it sounds stupid, but please just do this for me. You heard what Amanda said. Even though it may not be real to you it is to me, and I am afraid for Katie too," I explained.

"I am worried about you Melissa," Jake stated bluntly. "I don't know what to think and I really, really, hate lying to Katie!"

"I do too, Honey, I really do, but I cannot stress to you how important this is to me! Please try to understand. I have never asked you to do anything for me have I?" I pleaded.

"So how do we explain this to Katie? Jake shot back. How do we tell her that we took care of her doll and then it disappeared? Poof, gee Katie, we don't know what happened to your doll. Yeah we told you we would take care of her, *sorreeey!"*

"I got your point Jake! I will figure out something, just please do this for me," I woodenly replied.

Upon entering the house, I instantly felt the cold. I shuddered, and furtively looked around. Where was the little bitch hiding? I know I sound like I was paranoid. Well maybe I was, but I felt like I had cause to be. I quickly turned on the living room light, making me feel a little less fearful. There the little bitch sat. Staring at me from the couch, she sat woodenly, expressionless.

Her black eyes never blinked. Jake angrily lit the fire in the fireplace and when the flames shot up, he took Maude and held her in his hands, and said, "Sorry Maude, this one's for Melissa."

Maude did not reply. I really expected her to, but she lay just like a dumb rag doll. He tossed her in the fire, and she burned up without any fight. I felt stupid and relieved. There was no foul odor, which Jake quickly reminded me of.

"I hope now, Melissa, you can put the past behind you! I know what happened with you and that witch Maude was horrible. No child should have to go through that, the stalking and molestation is hideous and evil, but that was in the past. She is no longer real, and this was just a doll! So let's please put this foolishness behind us, and let the dead rest! Now let's try to think of a way to explain Maude's absence to Katie," Jake sighed.

Even though I felt relieved, I also felt ashamed, and sad. I thought that Jake was my protector, and when he talked to me that way, I felt so humiliated. I called Amanda that night and she reassured me. We talked about maybe getting a kitten or puppy for Katie to try to salve her wounds.

The best lie we could come up with is that Maude accidentally got mixed in with the dry cleaning when the cleaners came to pick up Jake's dress shirts. She would accidentally get ruined at the cleaners, and we would replace her with a live kitten or puppy of her choice. That was a small price to pay for freedom from evil.

Katie pranced in the house, happy as a little spring lamb. She quickly ran to find Maude. When I told her what happened she was crestfallen. "You said you would take care of her!" she wailed, heartbroken.

"Honey I am so sorry, the cleaners picked her up by accident," I tried to say sympathetically.

Now the hard part would be for her when Maude did not come back. I bet she would never trust the dry cleaners or me again. Small price I say.

I felt more relieved and lighthearted than I had in weeks. I called Amanda and told her how it had transpired. We could sleep in and not worry about Katie or her safety or mine. We went out to eat, and had a quiet night. We took a walk through the neighborhood, and saw the puppy in the neighbor's yard. Just the seed to sow Katie's desire for a pet, instead of a hideous clown doll. When we put her to bed that night, she cried for Maude, and I felt twinges of guilt. We tucked Tommy into bed with her. He was her rejected teddy bear, and told her that he would feel better too. That calmed her down and she went to sleep whimpering softly. Jake turned his back on me before going to sleep. Although I felt safer from Maude, I felt far from safe and protected by Jake. I felt sad and rejected, and worst of all, more than a little crazy.

Early morning sunlight spilled on my face, and I pulled the comforter down a little, warmed by the sun. I stretched and rolled over to look at my still dozing husband. He had taken a vacation day, and this was not a school day for Katie. We were going to have to face the last leg of Maude's disappearance today, but at least the dirty deed was nearly done.

"Do you forgive me Honey?" I asked Jake softly.

"Yeah, I do, I am sorry; I can't imagine what you went through. I just hate seeing Katie so upset, and I really hate lying to her," he said sincerely.

He spooned me and I felt loved and safe. It was beginning to look like a good day. I could feel him, against me, warm and hard, and I felt myself smile. "Feeling good today Honey?" I cooed.

"You feel real good!" He growled.

Just then I heard the patter of excited little feet. Katie bounded happily into our room and threw herself up on the bed. She excitedly screamed. "Look at what the cleaner man remembered! Maude is home and she is cleaner than ever!" She threw herself on top of us, and Maude was right with her.

I suppressed a scream of horror and revulsion. My eyes were wide with terror. I looked into Jake's face and he too looked like a rattlesnake had been tossed between us. Katie cooed and kissed Maude. I quickly slithered backwards off the bed.

"Katie, how do you know the cleaner's man brought Maude back? Where did you find her?" I cautiously asked.

"He left her on my bed Mama! Wasn't that nice of him?" He knew I missed her.

"Yes, Honey that was real nice of him," I replied more steadily than Jake looked.

"Let's get dressed and go out for breakfast, why don't we?" Jake shakily asked.

"My God, Melissa, what is going on?" Jake was white-faced and shaky.

"I don't know Honey, I honestly don't know. She said in court that she would pay me back, and that she was a black witch. That she would come back to haunt me for telling on her. Maybe she possessed the doll that is all I can say. But worst yet, how the hell do we get rid of her?" I whispered behind the bathroom door.

We quickly dressed and shouted for Katie to get ready, too. When we went down to her room, we didn't want to leave her alone with Maude. Katie looked troubled. She had lain back down on the bed and Maude was lying next to her. She was kissing Katie's neck. Katie was trying to push her away. Jake quickly grabbed Maude, and held her away from him at arms length. Katie was whimpering as she wiped her neck with a look of childlike disgust, like she was riding herself of a spider. I told her I would be right back that she should finish dressing. I closed the bedroom

door. Jake was holding the writhing thing out away from his body. It was hissing and spitting. He ran downstairs with it, and I ran into the kitchen for a plastic garbage bag. He tossed it in the fireplace and was just ready to light it, and I screamed at him, "No! Let's take it to Father Callahan!"

He slammed the door on the fireplace and it fought growled spat and hurled itself at the glass doors. Its eyes were wide open and the fires of hell burned in them. God what could we do?

I grabbed the crucifix off of the wall and held it up to the fireplace. Maude hissed and growled, but cowered in the back of the fireplace. I went up and got Katie, and told her that there was an emergency and that I was going to take her to the Jackson's next door and we would come and get her soon. I hurried her through the dining room. Jake was blocking her view. I could see the terror in his eyes as he held the crucifix up to the doors. I could hear her low growls.

Katie was white faced but unquestioning. I told Laura Jackson we had an emergency and asked if she could watch Katie. She said it would be a pleasure and asked no questions. I quickly ran back home.

"Father Callahan, please we need your help, can you please come to our house immediately?" I begged.

"I was just leaving, but I can come if it is an emergency." He formally answered.

"Please Father, it is an emergency," I stated.

"I will be there in ten minutes," he answered.

"Father, Wait! I need you to perform an exorcism," I stated bluntly. I hung up before he could question me.

I ran in the back door, and Jake was still standing there. He held out the crucifix and was repeating the Lord's Prayer. I grabbed my rosary and started reciting it with him. The thing continued to growl, lowly and would hurl itself toward the doors and hiss. Then she would retreat back and come back for more.

Father Callahan came in the front door and saw us standing in front of the fireplace, looking idiotic. In the fireplace lay a harmless doll. He looked at us in total confusion."What is the problem here guys?"

Jake would not look away from the fireplace, nor would he drop the crucifix. He explained everything to Father Callahan, shaking, with his hands gripping the crucifix.

"Father, I know you may think we are crazy. I didn't believe it could be true either. I even doubted Melissa when she told me she burned the bitch and it came back, but I saw it with my own eyes. She was lying there just like she is now to make me think that Melissa was crazy. But I saw her hissing and writhing earlier, and she came back! You have got to send it to hell Father, please!" Jake cried.

"Father, I whispered, you remember what happened to me and the neighborhood kids twenty years ago? Please you have got to help us, whether it is real to you or not, please exorcise this thing," I begged.

"Listen, I believe you, Maude McLane vowed that she would get even with you somehow, someday, and she admitted that she was a black witch and that we would come face to face one day. I don't talk openly about these things unless need be, but I believe you. She may not speak now, she is trying to make you look crazy, but I know better," Father Callahan explained.

Father took out the Holy water and his crucifix and Bible. He started praying and as he began to pray, Maude started screaming like a banshee. She battered against the glass; she spit and hissed, and growled, and beat on the sides of the fireplace. Father continued praying louder and we joined him. He literally threw Holy water through the fireplace doors and she railed and screamed and then he lit the fire and she burned and screamed and disappeared. He sent her to hell, and then blessed our entire house. We went through each room and opened each window and door. The fresh air streamed in and the sun shone brightly as he blessed each doorway, window and room. He prayed with us and listened to me as I told him about the shame and pain, and prayed over me and our family for healing and freedom from all evil. We even cleaned out the fireplace and sprinkled it with Holy water, and hung the crucifix back over the mantle.

After Father left, we prayed again, and Jake asked my forgiveness for doubting me. I forgave him and told him I understood why it was so hard for him to believe. I doubted myself. We went to pick up our darling little Katie. She was scared and ashen faced. She said she didn't want Maude back. That Maude scared her that morning. That she said some bad things to her and made her feel funny. We told her that Maude was gone and never coming back.

At McDonald's we watched Katie play and talked for a long time about our life and our goals. We thought about what was important, mainly our family and God. Katie came bounding over to us and we went out to the car. We stopped by the animal shelter and picked out the cutest little cocker spaniel mutt that you can imagine. I should say she picked us out. She came right up to Katie and licked her hand. Katie named her Maggie, a nice good Irish Catholic name.

Mathilda…A Living Doll

Many people have a fear of clowns and dolls. I admit I am one of them. I have never liked clowns. You never know what is hiding behind that make-up. We all remember John Wayne Gacy. I also have a fear of dolls. You never know when they may come to life. This is my story. It is one of the scariest things that I have ever experienced. I still can't believe that it really happened.

It was back in 1988. I was still recovering from a horrific divorce, reeling with pain and a shattered self-esteem. Out of desperation I started my own cleaning business. I had worked for the Baxter family for several years. They were always willing to accommodate my hectic schedule. Their house was beautiful with lovely big windows and sliding glass doors that overlooked a lazy, relaxing lake. I loved looking out of the windows as I cleaned their airy comfortable home. The sun would shine in brightly as I washed their windows and cleaned the luxurious rooms. I felt like I made their lives more comfortable. I felt appreciated and valued their friendship.

One morning when I came in the front door I was greeted by a new addition to their family. It was the vacuum cleaner with a cover standing in the corner of the entryway. I don't know if you have ever seen them. It was some sadist's idea of a craft or some weird art form. They look like a life-size doll that is meant to hide the ugly looking vacuum cleaner underneath. Instead it looks like a creepy life-size doll. When I would walk in the front door, there she stood. I would quickly remove her hideous self from the vacuum cleaner and stuff her in the coat closet.

One day, I don't remember why but I needed to come in the late afternoon instead of in the morning like I usually did. It was an eerie howling, bitter cold day. It was late fall and the leaves were beginning to fall and slither across the yards and streets. It was already beginning to get dark. Autumn crept in very quickly and I felt depression beginning to overtake me. That was the evening the unbelievable happened.

The Baxters went out to dinner and left me to my cleaning. The house was not as friendly or inviting, as it was in the bright sunlight in the daytime hours. The windows were black against the winter sky and the lake looked ominous and dark. The lights were dim and I felt a dread that I couldn't explain. I walked in looking toward the vacuum cleaner and saw that the hideous doll thing was missing. My first reaction was relief, my next feeling was panic. Where was she? I had started thinking of it as "she." I didn't want my imagination to get the best of me. I decided to work as fast as I could so I could get the hell out of there.

I got everything done upstairs and was ready to start cleaning on the main floor. I could picture Mathilda lurking around every corner. I could see her big black dead eyes leering at me. I could hear her maniacal whispering. I was working up a sweat as I worked in the family room. Where was she?

There were steps that led into the playroom in the basement. You could see the bar as you walked past the top of the stairs. I was cleaning the wood floor on my hands and knees and caught sight of Mathilda sitting at the bar downstairs. My breath caught and I felt my heart start to pound. How did she get down there? I saw her black curly yarn hair and her pink gingham dress. She was facing the mirror behind the bar. How did she get there? Was it Mark's idea of a joke? He, the man of the house didn't like Mathilda either. Maybe he put her there just to have a little fun.

Not funny! I didn't want to turn my back to her and started to rush through cleaning the floor. Don't be an idiot! I told myself. Just get the job done and get the hell out of here! Unfortunately the bad thing about having a vivid imagination and a creative mind is that it can begin to play tricks on you.

The wind began to howl and it was beginning to feel more and more like Halloween. It was only one week away. I heard the branches scraping the roof and I jumped. It was then that I heard it. I looked down the steps and Mathilda was no longer on the barstool. Where the hell was she? I must be losing my damned mind! I heard a thumping, slapping noise. Do you remember the bathtub scene in "The Shining?" Remember how that hideous naked corpse slapped across the floor? That was the noise I heard coming up the basement steps toward me. Then I saw it. She didn't have a real body you know.

She didn't have legs so she couldn't walk. She dragged herself up the steps, with her hideous misshapen hands. Her black yarn curls bobbed around her ghostly white fabric face. Her dead black huge round eyes leered at me. Her mouth was a puckered stitched "O" as she slobbered toward me. She was making mewling, whimpering sounds. Her gingham swathed bosom shuddered as she undulated toward me. I was immobilized, paralyzed with horror. My screams froze in my throat. I was on my hands and knees backing up away from her. She robotically thumped closer and closer. I could feel her putrid, vile breath on my neck. She began to reach out toward me with her mitten like hands. Her mouth stretched open, a yawning maw. The hideous black stitches that formed the "O" of her mouth pulled it into a grotesque grinning parody of a smile. It was then that I heard the front door open. Mark called out to me.

Mathilda slithered quickly back down the stairs. I sat rigid with fear. Mark said, "You look like you just seen a ghost. Ha, did you see I put that creepy doll thing downstairs by the bar? I am going to take her to the Goodwill tomorrow. She gives me the creeps."

"You don't say?" I whispered. "I think that would be a real good idea!"

If you ever go to the Goodwill or any place else for that matter, don't ever buy one of those creepy vacuum cleaner covers, especially one with black yarn hair, dead black eyes and a pink gingham dress.

A Friend for Sarah

Sarah felt sad, lethargic and lonely for a home that she never knew. When Sam told her that he had picked out a house for them in an established older neighborhood with beautiful older Victorian homes, she wanted to be happy and grateful. She loved Sam. He was the only man who ever had treated her with love and respect. Unfortunately all that she could feel was wooden and numb. Now that they were expecting their first child she wanted to be excited and happy. Instead she felt fearful and insecure. How could she take care of a baby when she didn't feel like she even had control over her own life? What kind of mother would she be?

Sam was ecstatic over the baby. That was when he decided to take control and pick out a house for them. She didn't mind because she really didn't know what she wanted. She was glad that he took control of the situation. She knew that she was lucky and that she should be grateful for a husband who loved her and was willing and able to work long hours to provide for her and a baby. She didn't have to work outside of the house, which was good because she knew that she wasn't very good at working with other people.

 She was glad that Sam took the initiative to introduce himself to her. She never would have been able to introduce herself to him or anyone else. Sam was her polar opposite. He never knew a stranger. He loved taking care of her and he was very positive. She had to fight depression, and lately she hadn't been doing a very good job of it. Yeah, it probably had to do with hormones and all, but it was worse than it had ever been.

The one thing that Sarah and Sam had in common was that they both loved antiques. When they first got married they explored the local and even some not so local antique shops and picked out furniture that they both loved. Now that they had everything that they needed it didn't take time to make the house comfortable.

On moving day Sarah didn't have to lift a finger. Sam wouldn't hear of it. The moving guys moved everything. The house had been cleaned, top to bottom, following Sam's instructions.

The Mighty Maids did a thorough job, whizzing in and out of the house in four hours. They even cleaned out all of the kitchen cabinets and put shelving paper in them too, for an added price. Sam was so excited that he gladly put the dishes and pots and pans in the cabinets, following Sarah's instructions. She really tried to be upbeat and excited. It would have helped if she had family to share this experience with. She didn't have any siblings and her drunken father was dead. Her mother, God only knew where she was. She had ran off and left Sarah with an ailing grandmother. Her grandmother died when Sarah was barely 18. She knew that her grandmother considered her a burden so she didn't even feel that great of a loss when she died.

Sam's family lived on the west coast. They breezed in for the small wedding and left within a couple of days. They were a lot like Sam, outgoing, friendly and personable. Sarah didn't feel very comfortable around them. They felt kind of overbearing to her. It was amazing that she married Sam considering how different that they were. Probably because Sam was so comfortable with taking control and she had such a hard time saying no, it wasn't that much of a surprise that she married him. If she were honest with herself she would have to admit that she liked being taken care of. It made it easy to stay home and to not have to be around other people that much. She was a little afraid that in time Sam might resent the fact that she didn't like having much of a social life. That was one of the reasons that she didn't complain when he played cards once a month with some of the guys from work.

Having a baby took off a little of the pressure to go out and make new friends. After a while Sam's friends quit asking them to come over for dinner or to go out. The baby now became a good excuse for not going out with friends. Sometimes, Sarah had morning sickness or didn't feel well. When the baby came that would also be a good excuse. She would worry about the rest later. With Sam being so excited about the baby it helped to divert his attention from the fact that they didn't have any friends together. In all honesty, Sarah didn't have any friends at all. Yes she got lonely, but it kept her life simple.

Decorating the baby's room also helped to keep her busy. She did get a little more excited because she had a knack for decorating. It was nice to do something with Sam too. He did the painting because of the paint fumes. He painted the walls a light mint green. The beautiful crown molding and trim he painted a gloss white. It was breathtaking. Sarah sewed curtains. She was torn about what kind to make because they didn't know if they were having a little boy or a little girl. She decided that Winnie the Pooh was perfect for either. Once the hard wood floor was polished they put a plush hunter green rug in the middle of the floor and the room was complete. The baby bed, bassinet and changing table gleamed white and ready for the new baby. The bay window overlooked the beautiful sunny backyard. She made pillows for the window seat and imagined reading to her baby in the near future.

After Sam and Sarah settled in, they began to establish a routine. There were only so many times that she could dust the furniture, vacuum and clean the house. Sarah began to get more restless. Sam was working long hours and she was lonely. When he was late for dinner on the night of her birthday she was really upset. He had promised to bring a cake home for her birthday. He wanted to take her out, but as usual she didn't want to go out to eat. He made up for his negligence by getting her a puppy for her birthday. He figured that it would be company for her and it would keep her occupied when he worked late. She named the butterscotch colored Cocker Spaniel, Rufus.

Sarah read every book and magazine that she could get her hands on. She weeded, planted and perfected every inch of the yard behind the house until she nearly lost her mind. She was upset because no one welcomed them to the neighborhood. Well, she saw Sam talk to that woman next door, but she never tried to talk to her. In all fairness she knew that she kept her distance and when the neighbor looked her way, she would keep her head down. After baking and cooking until she couldn't stand being in the house alone anymore and seeing the pleading look of longing on Rufus's face she decided out of sheer desperation to go for a walk.

Okay, poor Rufus was eating about as much as she was eating, out of sheer boredom. She knew she had to get him out for exercise and Lord knew she needed it too. If she went early in the morning or near dusk she was less likely to run into anyone.

She put Rufus on his leash and walked down the street, eyes straight ahead. The Victorian houses so similar to her own, stood like lady soldiers. Their colors were everything from lavender, yellow, and sage green to bright white with complimentary colored shutters. She loved the front porches with their wicker furniture and flowering plants. Geraniums rioted out of window boxes and brightly colored pots. Petunias, begonias and impatiens bloomed happily in the summer sun. She wanted so badly to talk to the women sitting on their porch swings sipping tea with each other. Her loneliness was only magnified by their sisterly camaraderie. She wished that she was outgoing and could just walk up and introduce herself. Occasionally she would hear someone's sparkling laughter spill behind her. She knew that they were laughing at her. Sometimes she thought she might hear someone call out to her or lift a hand in a wave, catching it out of the corner of her eye. She would just walk briskly by, lowering her head to whisper to Rufus. Maybe they wouldn't notice her.

One late afternoon she was feeling particularly isolated and lonely. Sarah walked with Rufus to the very end of Garden Street. There was a little bungalow house at the end of the wooded lot. It had a white picket fence around it. Well it used to be white. It needed painting, but then the house did too. She saw an old lady leaning on the gate watching her. She was to put it bluntly, fat. She looked bloated, unkempt and unattractive. She raised her hand up to Sarah and called out, "Hi Missy! New to the neighborhood?"

 Sarah shyly responded as she felt tears sting her eyes. "Yes we moved in late last spring." The old lady asked "Are you married?" "Yes, and we are having a baby in a few months."

"How about coming in for a little spot of tea?" the old lady invited. "Oh we couldn't impose. I have Rufus with me. He is pretty rambunctious," Sarah responded quickly. "Oh come on Missy don't be rude. You can leave the little beast outside. He can't hurt nothin' out here. Yard is a mess! I don't have time to keep it up anymore."Nobody comes to visit me. All these young people movin' inta the neighborhood. Don't have time for an

old lady like me!" she pouted. "Well okay for a few minutes I suppose it will be all right."

Sarah followed the old lady into the house. She shuddered as she watched her waddle over to the ancient looking stove. She tried to make herself comfortable at the little table that sat next to the window. The window was covered with old blinds. The blinds were coated with grime and dust. The room was closed up and smelled musty and dank. She felt the urge to run but couldn't make her legs move. She didn't want to be rude but promised herself that she would never come back to this hell house again.

The old lady creaked and groaned as she prepared tea on the old stove. She had a long kitchen match that she lit the burner with. Sarah watched as she pulled out tea cups from a broken down cabinet. She felt her stomach clench as the old woman began to ready the tea.

"What's your name Dearie?"

"Sarah and yours?"

"Mathilda, Mathilda Williams is my name."

"Are you married?"

"No Dearie, I have been by myself more years than I can count. Clem left me behind years ago. Died slowly right here in this house. Kids have long since moved away and left me to fend for myself."

"Oh I am sorry, I didn't mean to pry."

"Nonsense, Dearie. Them's been many years ago. I've gotten used to it. Living alone I mean."

They chatted amiably for some time. Sarah noticed that Mathilda was not well groomed. In fact she was downright slovenly. She was very bloated. Her hands and fingers were mottled. She had caked dirt on the hem of her skirts and the same dirt seemed to be embedded under her fingernails. She must have been working in the yard. You sure couldn't tell it by the looks of it though. She had an unpleasant sour odor clinging to her. Her hair was matted and tangled. Her eyes were almost colorless and Sarah noticed that she had whiskers growing out of her chin. She must be really desperate for a friend to want to spend time with this creepy old lady.

She made up her mind that she was never going to darken this old lady's door again. She could feel her skin crawl as the hair on the back of her neck rose. When she got up to leave, Sarah thanked Mathilda for the tea and company. When she opened the back door to walk out, Mathilda followed her. Rufus backed up, bearing his teeth. His hackles rose up, much like the hair on the back of Sarah's neck. He growled low in his throat and his whole little body began to shake as he backed up and tried to hide behind Sarah.

"Rufus! You stop that right now! What is wrong with you?" Sarah scolded with embarrassment. "He never acts like that!" In all fairness Rufus wasn't around strangers very often. But he really seemed to be overreacting. "Nonsense. The little beast will get used to me. He just doesn't know me. You come back and see me real soon, ya hear?"

Sarah thought fat chance. I might be desperate, but I am not that desperate. She noticed that the sun was beginning to slowly sink behind the trees. She hadn't even thought about dinner. Didn't really matter, Sam wouldn't be home until late tonight anyways. It was his poker night. She enjoyed having someone to talk to, but Mathilda was, to put it bluntly, repulsive. She shuddered to herself thinking back on the tea that she drank. Come to think of it, she didn't drink any tea!

What? She saw Mathilda pour the tea. She was trying not to be impolite, but there was no tea in her cup? Or was there? Oh well it didn't matter, she was never going back there again!

When she got home she took a long hot bath. She wanted to wash away every remnant of the time that she spent with Mathilda. She even rinsed out her nose. She could still smell the stink of the old woman and her house. For some odd reason, she didn't tell Sam about visiting Mathilda. She felt almost a quiet shame about visiting her. Maybe it was because Mathilda was old and odd. He had encouraged her to make women friends her own age. He knew that there were women in the neighborhood. There was a very nice lady their age right next door. She noticed that he didn't have a problem leaning on their fence talking to her! When Sam would be outside on the weekend she would see him go over and talk to Sandy. He told Sarah that her name was Sandy. The more he tried to get her to talk to her the less she wanted to. Sarah was getting bigger with the baby and feeling fat, bloated and unattractive. Sure enough here comes Sam talking to that woman again. She just came outside around the corner of the house and there he was smiling and laughing! She hadn't heard him laugh with her in months! She was afraid that they had spotted her and she backed up against the side of the house. Slowly she sneaked back into the kitchen. When Sam came in he said that Sandy wanted to meet her.

Sarah spat out at him. "Seems she doesn't need to talk to me when she has you all to herself!" Sam just walked away shaking his head at her. When they were in bed that night, Sarah rolled over and wouldn't even kiss him goodnight. She made plans to go back to Mathilda's again the next day. As much as she tried she couldn't stay away. It had been a week since she had visited with Mathilda.

As repulsed as she was by Mathilda, it was like a magnet pulled her back to the dark pit. The contrast between Mathilda's house and presence and the light of the other neighbors was palpable. Rufus had to be dragged into the yard. He would quiver and shake until she came back out of Mathilda's. Sarah would feel a sense of shame leaving him there and more so for going there herself. Depression was beginning to weigh her down. Maybe it was the thought of the baby coming and all the responsibility that went with it. She felt as big as a house. Then she would see Sandy next door with Tom, her handsome husband, talking to Sam over the backyard fence. She was sure that they were talking about her. When Sam tried to introduce them to her she was furious. She didn't need to meet them. They were stuck up and they didn't want to talk to her. They only wanted to be friends with him. She told him that she made her own friend. She proudly told him that she made friends with a very kind older lady that lived at the end of Garden Street.

"Garden Street?" Sam asked with a puzzled expression on his face. "There isn't anyone living at the end of Garden Street. There is only that old bungalow house that is up for sale there," Sam added. "It isn't for sale! Mathilda lives there. Her husband has been dead for years, but she lives there by herself. The neighbors ignore her too. She is very nice to me! I don't need your stuck up friends!" Sarah exploded.

Sam just looked at her quizzically. He didn't say another word, but he was getting a little worried. He knew that Sarah was more introverted, but lately she seemed to be getting more and more withdrawn. She came home from walking Rufus one afternoon when he got home early and asked her where she had been. Rufus was quivering and nervous, not like when he took him out for walks. He asked her where she had been and she said she had been out for a walk, thank you.

What was that smell? Sam was gripped with an overwhelming urge to throw up. It seemed to be permeating Sarah's clothes and hair. He was glad when she promptly went in to take a bath. It

was a perfect time to take Rufus outside for a bath. He smelled like he had rolled in something dead. Sarah was so mad that she was spitting nails. Damn him! Here she was big as a house, needing his attention and he was talking to that damned Sandy again. She stalked out the front door with Rufus in tow. Even Rufus was annoying, whining again. He acted like he didn't even like taking walks with her anymore.

She was determined that she wasn't going to Mathilda's and yet here she was, feet stomping in the direction of the old crone's house. When she got in front of the house she saw a "For sale" sign in the yard. There had to be a mistake. There stood Mathilda looking at her from the back yard fence.

"Why is your house up for sale Mathilda? You said that you weren't selling," Sarah asked petulantly.

"I am not selling this house! Them damned little brats are pulling a prank on me! They will have to take me out of my house feet first! Come on in and sit a spell with me Missy. Rest your bones, looks like you might explode. Don't want that baby to come too soon." Mathilda cooed.

"Oh, I am so mad at Sam I could kill him! He thinks I don't have eyes! He was talking to that skinny little bitch in her halter top and shorts right in front of me! She thinks just because I am pregnant she can get my husband. I should have known! Men are all alike. Just like my dad!

God, I hate him. She had the gall to smile at me right when she was flirting with my husband! I hate her and I hate him too!" Sarah was fuming.

"Come on now Dearie. Settle yourself down and you little beast, stay outside." Mathilda soothed Sarah while glaring at Rufus. Sarah was still fuming over Sam. "He thinks I don't have eyes? He thinks I can't see him lusting over that little bitch! God I hate him!"

"Calm yourself down Dearie. I have a little something for you and the baby. You know men are all alike. A leopard can't change its spots. I know I had one of my own. He had to learn the hard way I am afraid. I taught him a lesson. There are ways you know. Little spot of tea every day makes things right. He learned what happens when you stray." Mathilda was in her own little world as she sing-songed to Sarah.

Sarah was still so angry that she didn't notice what was going on right in front of her eyes. She listened to Mathilda, hypnotized. "Come on Dearie. I have something for you upstairs."

Sarah didn't notice the cold bloated, lichen slickened hand on her shoulder. She didn't notice until late, too late, the stench emanating from the swollen body as she woodenly started up the old plan k stairs to the bedroom on the upstairs floor. She noticed the wallpaper, mildewed and water -stained in the stairwell. She felt trapped as the thing closed in on her on the steps. There was no way out. She heard the slap of the dead cold feet clump on the steps behind her. Terrified to turn around, but she had to, she whirled and there was Mathilda. Her eyes were like wet cold hard boiled eggs. There were no irises. The stench made her stomach roil. Mathilda reached for her, her hands like bloated white hams, rotting fingers trying to knead her flesh. Screams rose out of Sarah's throat. Blood curdling screams as Mathilda, mewled and panted toward her. She could feel the swampy cold breath on her face as she scrambled to get away from her. There was no place to run. Sarah's belly clenched and water gushed from between her legs as she collapsed helplessly under the dead grotesque legs of Mathilda. Her world turned black as she felt her gorge rise in her throat.

Sam was beginning to worry. He'd noticed that something about Sarah didn't look right. She also looked pissed as hell. He told Sandy that he thought he needed to go try to find her. He was really pissed off at her too. This was getting ridiculous. He was going to have to get professional help for her. Call it God or just intuition, he drove down Garden Street. He saw the "For Sale" sign leaning on the brown grass. The gate was hanging open and the fence was falling apart. Rufus was cowering in the corner of the yard. Panic assailed him. Oh my God where was Sarah?

Without hesitation he ran in the back door and was overcome by the vilest stench of human death. It was an odor once smelled one never forgot. He started to gag, but panic and fear was uppermost in his mind. He followed the stench. The door to an upstairs was standing open. He heard Sarah screaming as if the devil himself was after her, perhaps he was. She was doubled over trying to protect their baby in her belly. What he saw for just a split second was something that he would never forget. It was something that would haunt his nightmares for the rest of his life. It was salivating and leering as it turned its head toward him. Eyes, like rotting boiled eggs, sightless, yet seeing into his very soul. Just as he saw it, it was gone.

He held his breath as the overpowering stench assailed his nostrils. Sarah's terror filled eyes were riveted to the ceiling of the stairwell, where she could see the corpse of Mathilda swinging from a rope. Then it was gone. Sam scooped her up and ran with her to the car. Rufus followed whining as he jumped into the back seat. Sarah was doubled over in pain as Sam drove her to the hospital after dropping Rufus off at home. Neither one of them could speak.

Sarah was in shock, but then so was Sam. Her labor was hard but little Max was born, squalling, red-faced and healthy. They both looked at him in wonder and amazement. Everything that had happened that afternoon seemed like a bad nightmare. They knew that it would take a long time to process what they had both experienced that day, but for the time being they wanted to focus on their new baby boy.

The next day Sandy came to the hospital with flowers and a present for baby Max. She told Sarah that she had always been shy too and found it hard to approach her. She wanted to be her friend and hoped that they could get to know each other. Sarah realized that she wasn't the only one who had problems. She had no idea that Sandy suffered too.

Sam and Sarah became friends with Sandy and her husband Tom. They joined a neighborhood association and began to have barbeques and play dates with other families with children. Sandy and Sarah would walk with their babies and Rufus too. Little Mandy was born just 6 months after Max. In time Sarah told Sandy a little about the experience that she had with Mathilda and why she never wanted to walk down Garden Street.

It was chilling to hear that the reason the empty house on Garden Street had never sold was because the old lady that lived there, named Mathilda had slowly poisoned her husband to death. After he died she was found hanging in her upstairs stairwell. Rumor had it that sometimes people thought that they saw her in her yard leaning on her picket fence. But then you know the stories that people tell.

A Lover for Jenna

Jenna felt an inexplicable loneliness. It haunted her since the death of her husband Gary. They had been married for only three years. Although the newness had worn off and they knew each other's habits and likes and dislikes very well, their passion was still very much alive. Maybe it had to do with the fact that they didn't have children and they both loved their careers. Yet when the week was over so were their responsibilities. They spent the weekends together. They would go to mass and out to eat, doing various things together that they both loved. It really wasn't unusual for them to spend long hours in bed together on the weekend. Jenna loved waking up in the middle of the night, throwing her leg over Gary's and spooning him, melding to his body. They fit together perfectly. She loved to feel his sleep warmed body and deep contented breathing.

When Jenna got the call that there had been an accident, she was worried, but never expected that Gary was taken to the hospital. Dr. Mueller met her in the hall and he gravely told her that Gary's condition was very serious. She stood next to his bedside, numb with horror, grief already crawling up her throat. They called her parents, and they all tried to support her best that they could but after two days a decision had to be made. She couldn't make him suffer for her sake. She didn't want to let him go, but she knew that it would be selfish of her to make him go on for her. Tears streamed down her frozen cheeks. Yes, she would donate his organs. Yes he would be cremated. Yes, he had a living will. She kissed him one last time and they gave her the time she needed to say her good-byes to him.

She lay in bed next to him and cradled him in her arms; his body was already unfamiliar to her. He was cold and unresponsive. She whispered in his ear to him. She told him how much she loved him and how she didn't want to let him go. She begged him to come back to her, and railed at him for leaving her. Her mother heard her wailing and came to her. She held her as she fell to her knees, sobbing. She had to let him go. She was then able to tell him that he should go to God and that she would meet him there someday.

Days turned to weeks, weeks turned into months. Each week was a repeat of the last. Jena moved woodenly through her workweek, and faced the weekends with dread. If the workweek was bad, the weekends were torture. She turned away from the help of her family and friends. Gary was all that she needed, and all that she wanted. No one could comfort her. She was full of rage with God for killing Gary. She didn't care what anyone said, she blamed God. God could have stopped it. Why didn't he save Gary? With all the murderers, child molesters, and monsters out there, why, oh why God, did you have to let Gary die? Why not kill some of those sons-of-bitches? There was no answer, and no understanding.

Once again she lay in bed full of grief and bitterness. She was not expecting to feel hotness and need inside her. She wasn't expecting to feel lust and desire. She was disgusted with herself. How could she be feeling sexual desire, when her husband was dead? She tried to go to sleep with the television on as usual but tossed and turned. Finally she fell into a fitful sleep. She sighed softly, turning and cuddling up to him. She wrapped her leg around his warm body, and nuzzled her nose into his neck. She began to run her tongue up the back of his neck. Her body was on fire, and her face flushed, her warm, wet mouth burning for him. She caught his earlobe between her teeth and began to suckle it. Oh God, it was real, he was back with her! She pressed herself into him.

Then she began to feel him. His body was cold, stone cold, and hard. What was that God-awful smell that taste? She began to wretch pulling herself away as she shuddered with revulsion. She turned over and grabbed for the nightlight switch. She turned it on, gasping, she turned, and there was nothing there! Oh God, what was happening to her? She could still feel the cold clamminess against her skin. She shuddered and gagged. Running for the bathroom, she made it just in time to throw up in the toilet. She convulsed and threw up until she couldn't throw up anymore. Sliding to the floor, she held on to the toilet seat, trembling with weakness and horror.

What was wrong with her? She would have sworn that Gary was with her. Her cheeks flamed as she remembered her passion and lust for him. She woke up with the stench and horror of death next toher and thought that she was crazy. She would not tell anyone about it. They would think she was insane. Maybe she was.

Time marched on and she continued doing what she always did. She wouldn't go out with the girls and when her parents wanted her to come over she would postpone until later. She kept to herself and watched home videos of her and Gary. She cried herself to sleep every night and railed at God for torturing her.

One Saturday morning she decided she had had enough. She went to the Health Club and worked out with a vengeance. She decided that she was not going to turn into a vegetable. When she left she saw a guy watching her reflection in a plate glass window. She felt a rush of lust run through her body.

She felt like her old self as she walked taller and her breasts began to tingle. She felt hot and horny. She would not give into it. This was ridiculous! The problem with her working out and eating better was that she was also beginning to feel lustful and sexual again. She couldn't find satisfaction like some of her friends talked about, but she found herself fantasizing again about Gary. Sometimes she would see a guy that turned her on and she would try to stop herself from thinking about him and what she could do to him and vice versa.

Jenna had the old familiar dream again. She melded herself against the hot firm body in bed. Her breath was hot and raspy with lust. She slid her hand down between his legs and gasped at the hot hardness there. She caught her breath and continued doing what was instinctive. He in turn lit her body on fire. She never felt this even in life. She was wild and abandoned herself to the pleasure and fullness that he gave her. When she opened her eyes he was gone but the smell was there. It was that gagging smell of death. She rushed to the bathroom and threw up. My God what was happening to her? She felt the evidence of what had happened and she saw the line of hickeys all up and down her neck and on her breasts, and everywhere else. She was repulsed when she saw the teeth marks and blood that was drying on her thighs. It wasn't a dream? It wasn't Gary? Oh God what was it? What was happening to her?

Jenna was beginning to miss work. Her eyes were dark hollows and her friends were getting worried about her.

"Jenna, are you feeling all right?" Traci asked her.

"No, I don't feel well, but I am going to the doctor." Jenna lied. She couldn't go to the doctor. What would she tell him? "Hey Doc, I have been having the wildest sex of my life and I don't know who with. I don't even think it is real! My husband is dead but something is pouncing on my bed at night and making me crazy with lust. When I wake up my body is covered in bites and I am anemic. I don't want to lose the sex but I am terrified. I smell death and the sheets are dank and wet from decomposing flesh. Is there a cure for this? Even my dog won't come in the room anymore. She cowers in the living room and won't let me pet her on mornings after this happens." Jenna fantasized telling the Doctor this.

When she got on the scales one morning before work she weighed only 94 pounds. She had lost 40 pounds! God she always wanted to lose weight but she looked at herself in the mirror and she looked like a concentration camp victim. When she took her t-shirt off and looked in the mirror her body was covered with bloody scratches and bites. She dressed hurriedly after showering the stench of death off of her ravaged body. She put on a heavy turtleneck to cover the bites and blood on her neck.

She lay in bed exhausted and terrified. Her hopelessness was like a shroud. She called out to God and to Gary. Oh Gary I am so sorry I know it isn't you. I thought it was, I wanted you so badly, but I know it wasn't you. You would never hurt me, please, take this away!

She woke up from dreaming with tears streaming down her gaunt face. Gary told her that he loved her and held her in his arms. He kissed each damaged area of her body gently. She lay limp in his arms and felt the warmth of his body and love. She never wanted it to end. She was terrified and lonely. Gary was the only thing that she wanted and he made her feel safe again.

"Jenna you have got to get help. I know you are angry with God for taking me away. I can't explain why He took me away either. But I love you and I always will. I want you to be happy. Someday we will be together again. A demon is attacking you. He is killing you. Please go to Father James and he will help you. Don't be embarrassed it is not your fault." Gary gently but firmly spoke to her.

She fell back to sleep for the first time without fear. She made a decision to see the Priest. She was still angry with God but she needed help. The next morning she made an appointment to see Father James. She felt Gary with her as she tried to tell the Priest the humiliating story about what was happening to her. The horror that she saw on his face when he saw her told her that he believed her. She pulled the neck of her sweater down to her shoulder. He could see the bites and bruises all up and down her neck.

"Father I am so sorry I haven't been back to church since Gary was killed. I was so angry with God! I still am. But I am getting past it I think. Please help me I don't know what to do." Jenna pleaded.

Trying to cover his revulsion over what at happened to her; Father James anointed her while praying for her protection and the deliverance of the evil that possessed her.   He told her that he and Father

John who was familiar with demonic possession would come to her apartment and cleanse it. He had to get together with the other priest and make plans.

Jenna thanked him and for the first time had a little hope that she could be rescued. She had breakfast at a little corner bakery and went home. She read and took a hot bath and pampered her wasted body. She lit candles and read until she was sleepy. She blew the candles out and held her crucifix in her hands against her heart. She covered herself with freshly washed sheets and fell instantly to sleep.

Jenna felt it! It pounced on the bed. It was snarling and gnashing its teeth. It was angry! It was full of rage. She cringed and cried out to God but it pulled the sheets back and saw the crucifix. It lunged for her and tossed the hot crucifix to the floor. She fought and valiantly tried to protect herself. Shestarted praying and it just laughed. It had a hideous, evil laugh that rolled through its whole decaying body. It smelled of death. It plunged itself into her as she screamed and screamed and screamed.

When she awoke she couldn't move. She was paralyzed and her body was so weak she couldn't get out of bed. Father James was worried about Jenna and he and Father John met at her apartment building. She didn't answer the telephone or the door. Father James kicked the door in. Jenna was not moving. Her bed was covered with blood. Her dog was cowering under the sofa in the living-room. She was breathing but barely. Father James called an ambulance and her parents. When her parents arrived to go with her to the hospital they gasped in horror. They thought she had been murdered.

After they left, Father James and Father John went to work. They performed a cleansing ritual and blessed the apartment. That night when they got the news that Jenna was going to live they performed a cleansing ritual on her in the hospital. Jenna told them that Gary was with her and she felt that he had saved her life the night of the final attack.

Jenna was able to go to the cemetery where Gary's ashes were buried. She put flowers on his tombstone and lay a crucifix on the top of it. She felt the familiar pain but also felt at peace for the first time since Gary's death. The first ray of hope for a future began to fill her heart.

She and her dog Princess went to stay with her parents until she was recovered. She gave up the lease on her apartment. She wanted a clean slate. Princess again slept with Jenna, which let Jenna know that there was no evil spirits after her anymore. She was looking forward to moving on with her life again without any spirits, at least not any evil spirits anyway.

Christmas at Aunt Delphie's

Christmas at Aunt Delphie's was always something special. You see she had these dolls that looked as though they were alive. I was just a little girl in the 1950's. I don't know if you remember what dolls from that period looked like back then. One of my favorites had dark hair and brown eyes just like mine. Her eyes would open and shut and she had real eyelashes. When you picked her up she would say, "Mama." I loved her and named her Mattie that is until the last Christmas that we went to Aunt Delphie's.

I didn't mention the part about the teeth. I guess that is because that is the worst part about what happened at Aunt Delphie's. I took Mattie with me wherever I went. Do you remember how dolls back then had teeth? Mattie had teeth too. They looked real in her little red lipped mouth. You could even see a hint of tongue behind her teeth. It wasn't until that last Christmas at Aunt Delphie's that I thought of it as anything ominous and menacing.

I will now tell you the most horrifying experience of my life during the Christmas season of 1955. I was 6 years old and still believed in Santa Claus and the tooth fairy. I was a little bit suspicious of the tooth fairy, but I still believed in Santa Claus. I could hardly wait to get to Aunt Delphie's. Our whole family was going to be there and Santa would bring us lots of presents on Christmas Eve.

We pulled up in front of the house as the snow whirled around us. It was magical. I bounded out of the car with all the enthusiasm of a 6-year-old believer in Santa Claus. I clutched Mattie to my chest, feeling the joy and excitement of being with my little cousins and relatives.

The Christmas lights bloomed through the large snowflakes as they lit up the front porch of Aunt Delphie's Victorian house. The parlor was decorated with every kind of Christmas decoration you can imagine. The air was fragrant with the smell of pine. The Christmas tree top just grazed the ceiling with its peaceful little angel that I knew that Aunt Dephie handmade. She had decorated the tree with captivating little ornaments all handmade by her. The tree was breathtaking.

The smells of cooking and baking tantalized my taste buds. I could smell ginger and cinnamon. The aroma of turkey and ham wafted through the air. Those are the memories I try to cling to while I write about the horror of that Christmas season.

Aunt Dephie made dolls. Her walls had handcrafted shelves and cases made just for her dolls by her husband, Uncle George. She also collected other dolls that she displayed with her handmade ones. It was fascinating to look at them. They looked like real little people and babies. Sometimes I would almost believe they were real. Their eyes would glisten and shine. I would stare at them for so long that I would get the creeps. I would go into another room where the dolls would no longer be staring at me.

That night still had all the magic and joy of the previous Christmases. We ate until we could hardly move and then it was time for Santa to bring our presents. I wondered why he brought them on Christmas night but I didn't question them. It seems they told us that because he had so much to do on Christmas Eve we were lucky that he made a special trip to Aunt Delphie's to bring us our presents first. We tore into the presents and played until it was time for bed. I was thrilled that Santa had brought me all the things that I asked for. I got a little sister for Mattie that I promptly named Mandy. She was a carbon copy of Mattie but she was smaller.

Christmas morning was full of the same magic as the night before. We ate all day and played until we were exhausted. We were going to spend the night again and leave the next morning. We had slept upstairs with our parents on Christmas Eve night but wanted to have a little slumber party downstairs before we had to get ready to leave in the morning.

It felt like a real adventure for us to be able to sleep downstairs away from the adults. There were seven cousins in all including me that would spend the night on the floor across from the parlor. It was beautiful to be able to see the lights from the Christmas tree. We had our little sleeping bags littering the carpeted floor. My younger cousins were so tired that they nearly passed out as soon as their heads hit their pillows. Each little body was curved into little commas or sprawled out like dolls on their backs. I being the oldest was having a hard time falling asleep from the excitement. I had Mattie and Mandy both in my arms as I lay facing the Christmas tree in the parlor. The Christmas tree lights glowed warmly as I tried to soothe myself to sleep.

All the adults were upstairs already sleeping in their beds. I am sure they were exhausted from cleaning the dinner remains. They were stuffed with food and the turkey made them somnolent. I could hear my Daddy snoring as the house settled into peace.

It was then that I saw it. First I thought my eyes were playing tricks on me. The little dolls on the Christmas tree started to move. I lay as still as a mouse. I held my breath. The tree began to rustle. Then the dolls on the shelves started moving. Their eyes opened and clicked from side to side. I was paralyzed with terror. I could hear a soft tittering and whispering. I heard their little teeth began to chatter. I was afraid to move but looked down at Mattie and Mandy. Their eyes shot open and their teeth were clicking. I pushed them away from me with revulsion.

The other dolls began to lumber stiff-legged from the parlor toward us. Eyes rolling, teeth clacking and simpering, little mewling noises were emitting from their little bloody mouths. I lay rigid with terror. They began to attack---- biting, hissing and tearing the flesh off of my little cousins. They didn't make a sound. They just lay there. Blood was everywhere. I could feel their teeth sinking into me. I tried to scream as I watched my little cousins lay motionless. I screamed and screamed and screamed, silently. The harder I tried to scream the less effectual I became.

I still can see their eyes and teeth as they pulled and tore at our flesh. They were like rabid dogs. I don't know how long it lasted or how it stopped. I can still see the bloodied bodies of my little cousins lying on the floor and feel my own body throbbing in pain as the flesh on my body was torn away, blood pouring from every bite.

I remember that everything went black. The morning sun poured in the windows and I could smell bacon frying. I could hear my mother laughing with Aunt Delphie. My father walked past us out the front door to grab a smoke outside. I looked around and saw my cousins rousing from sleep. The dolls were all back in their places. Mattie and Mandy were cuddled up next to my body. There was no evidence of the night's previous horror. I could still feel the pain from the bites but couldn't see the proof. I was stunned by the normalcy.

Woodenly I got in to the car for the journey home. I conveniently forgot Mattie and Mandy. My mother and father wanted to know what was wrong with me. I told them that I had a horrible nightmare. They laughed and said it must have been all the food we had eaten.

When I took my bath that night my mother asked me why I had teeth marks on the back of my neck. I told her it must have been from my cousin Susie. She loved to bite. If it wasn't from Suzie it must have been from the doll attack. She laughed and said it must have been from my nightmare.

I know you are probably wondering if we went back the next Christmas. Aunt Delphie died that spring. It was really a very sad time but a relief to me because I didn't have to go back there for Christmas ever again.

I write this from a mental hospital. You see Aunt Delphie willed all her dolls to my mother and me.

She Loves Me She Loves Me Not

Maria loved Thomas passionately. Some may have called it obsessively. But then maybe they were never really in love. Maria learned from her parents what real love was all about. Unfortunately with that kind of love bad things happen. When Maria's mother found out that her husband was having an affair with her best friend, well let's just say it ended badly. Maria was a bitter orphan.

Maria inherited the house from her parent's after their untimely deaths and promptly moved in with her sparse belongs. Since the master bedroom was roomy and faced the lake she decided that in spite of the horrible happenings in that room that she wanted to make it her own. Thomas and she had been married a short period of time and she didn't feel that it was necessary to tell him about her parents grisly end. During their short courtship all was passion and romance.

She refurnished and redecorated the bedroom before they moved in. New carpet was a necessity. The walls also needed to be recovered with new wallpaper after the damage was repaired. There was no way that the stains would come out of the beautiful hardwood floors, which was a damned shame. She really loved the oak floors. Maria was practical though and had the floor covered with new carpet.

The furniture must stay though. She loved the heavy oak furniture and the standing mirror that her mother had spent many hours in front of needed to remain. She remembered being a little girl admiring herself in the mirror in her mother's gowns and high heels. Lying on the bed she could see their reflections in the mirror as she and Thomas made love. Thomas was everything to her, just like Daddy was to her mother.

Maybe sleeping in their parent's bedroom would have bothered some people, making love with their spouses. It didn't bother Maria though. It didn't even bother her that her mother had murdered her father in the same room. What did bother her was that Thomas started staying out late many nights. He would come home drunk and she smelled another woman on him. He of course denied it. After having him followed though, her worst suspicions were true.

Maria felt bile and rage well up in her throat. She knew how to deal with the betrayal though. Her mother had taught her well. As Thomas lay sleeping in a stupor, she hacked him to pieces with her mother's axe. Getting rid of the evidence was the hard part. It was quite a chore to have to cut him up and feed him to the fishes in the lake. Bones don't burn very well in a fireplace. It took her over a week to get rid of him. When she was finished though she was able to clean up the bedroom and change the bedding and all was well.

Ironically Maria was a clean freak. She was really infuriated by the little dark spot that she had to keep rubbing off of the mirror. Her mirror was her pride and joy as it was a family heirloom. It still hurt when she thought of the many times that she and Thomas had made love and she could see their reflections in the mirror. Now it only brought back painful memories. She was still haunted by his betrayal.

Maria would wake up in the morning and the spot that she removed the day before on her beautiful mirror would be back. Each day it seemed to grow a little more. She would clean it frantically and the next day it would be back. Was it a defect in the glass? One morning she noticed that it had become even larger and began to take on an ominous shape. No it couldn't be but it seemed to take on the shape of a blood splatter. She couldn't take it in to be replaced. What if someone became suspicious? Already some were asking about where Thomas had gone.

Maria turned the mirror to the wall and slept fitfully. Six months to the day that she had murdered her husband she awoke to see the mirror facing her. In hideous Technicolor, the mirror replayed the murder that she had committed in front of her eyes. Thomas's face in all of its horror leaped out at her from her beloved mirror.

When the maid came in a week later she found Maria dead in bed. The stench was awful. The look of terror on her face was one that her maid would never forget. The room although pristinely clean reeked of death. The mirror stood an innocent sentinel to the horror before it. After the funeral, the Realtor had the house cleaned and put it up for sale, all furnishings were included.

The Monster in Billy's Closet

Billy was the best little boy in the world. He had to be. His life with his mother and stepfather was a nightmare. Only this nightmare lasted every day and every night. He loved his mother. But she may as well not have been there at all. She drank that yucky smelling stuff all the time and sat like one of those zombie things in the dark living room, day and night. You know the kind on those scary movies. His mother and stepfather liked to watch those movies. Sometimes it was hard to tell which was which because they looked like the zombies in the movies. Only Butch was much scarier. At least he could get away from the ones in the television.

He didn't know how to treat Butch, or even what to call him. If he called him Butch, he would scream, "God damnit! Call me Daddy you little ungrateful shit! Who do you think pays for all the shit that you eat? I put a damned roof over your worthless mother's head and yours! Don't forget it, you fuckin little asshole!"

If Billy called him Daddy, Butch would scream, "Don't you call me Daddy, you fucking little turd! I'm not your fucking Daddy! Who knows who that fucking son of a bitch your whore mother was with! Anyone could be your Daddieeee!"

So mostly little Billy would try to avoid calling him anything at all. He just tried to stay out of his way. Everything he did was wrong. He would try to sneak food from the refrigerator. That was hard, because it was close to the living room and that was where Butch was most of the time. If he ate with them, Butch would backhand him as sure as look at him. So not only did his head hurt, so did his empty little stomach. Usually the only thing that he could find in the refrigerator was dried up old cold meat.

On the rare occasions that he got to go stay at his grandma's house, he would eat until he was sick. Grandma loved him and she was the only safe person in his life. He tried not to cry when he came back to Butch's house, because he would be called a God damned baby. He would scuttle to his room, trying to make himself smaller than he already was. Four year-old boys aren't very big. He only had a small bed with a thin mattress on it. He was ashamed because if Butch caught him trying to clean up the mess, he would make him sleep naked and shivering in the cold bare little room. Life was unbearable for Billy. Just when he thought it couldn't possibly get worse, it did. He was used to Butch coming in with his horrible pukey-breathe and lying in bed with him. He turned inside himself. There was no place to hide. He would imagine that he was at Grandma's house laying in the grass with the warm sun shining on him. He would be full and safe. But even in his fantasy he had tears sliding down his face.

He was sure that he must have cancer or something awful like Grandpa had before he died. When he would go to the bathroom, his little butt would bleed and he hurt so badly that he could hardly walk. Billy hated Butch with a loathing that was beyond anything that he could imagine in his head. This is when he began to hear the monster in the closet.

At first he thought it was just a rat. They had plenty of them in the house. It would rustle and thump in the closet. He huddled in his thin sheet, his heart pounding like the sound of the ocean's roar. Never mind that he had never been to the ocean. He tried to tug on Mama and get her to come and protect him. But Mama was always like one of the zombies, dark eyes, glazed over or shut. Out of sheer desperation he once asked Butch to come and check out the closet. He did that only once. Butch did what Butch always did. The monster was safer.

Billy would try to sleep at night. He no longer tried to get anything out of his closet. Not that there was anything in there to get. He had a few thin shirts and pants in a broken down dresser drawer. He had found a couple of broken and discarded action figures in the alley that he hid under the bed. Butch wasn't going to have any kid of his playing with dolls! Mostly he just tried to be invisible.

He heard the growling, bumping monster every night when he tried to disappear or go to sleep. He never got used to it. He figured that maybe the monster was hungry and if he fed it, it would go away. He would sneak in the kitchen after Butch had eaten and was passed out on the couch, and get some cold meat. Even though his little belly was still growling, he would throw half of it into the closet. He would scurry as fast as a mouse and jump back in his bed. He hoped that this might keep the monster away from him when he tried to sleep.

The sad thing was that as scared as he was of the monster, he was more scared of Butch. Butch would tease him about the monster in the closet. He had learned a long time ago not to try to get help from Butch with the monster or anything else for that matter. His mother may as well not be there at all.

The only thing that she was good for was a punching bag for Butch. Sometimes he would hear them in the bedroom. Butch would make the same noises that he did when he came to Billy's room at night. It made him sick and he would cover his ears and try to block the sounds from his ears.

Billy started being less afraid of the monster. He began to take a little longer tossing the meat into the closet. He even called the monster a name. He called him Angel. What a strange name for a monster, but somehow it was the only thing that Billy could count on to be there for him. He pictured how it looked. It didn't look like the pictures that he had seen of angels though. He knew that it was big. He even got a little glimpse of it a couple of times. It had red slanted eyes. It was hairy and it smelled like a wet dog. He was sure that it had black long hair. Its teeth were huge and pointed. He heard it making slurping noises after he threw the meat in the closet.

After Butch left his room at night, Billy found himself talking to the monster. He would cry silently, with soft hiccupping sobs. He asked the monster why Butch hurt him and hated him so."Angel, why am I so bad? I try to be good, but I must be horrible. My mother doesn't love me. Butch hurts me and makes fun of me all the time. He killed my puppy Blackie. I don't have any friends. I am hungry and cold all the time. I wish I was dead," Billy would whisper.

One night as Billy lay pretending to be asleep, Butch came in his room. He was ready for a fight. He needed someone to humiliate and berate, and who better than Billy?

"Ooooh Billy, is the big bad monster in your closet tonight?" Butch slurred and danced with his ugly hairy beer belly bloating out from under his disgusting dirty wife beater. I want to *seeee* the mean old monster in your closet!! Come here big scary monster! Have a little wee snack! Billy isn't much to eat. I can promise you that!" He evilly leered at Billy.

Billy cowered under his wet sheet. Afraid to breathe, he feigned sleep. He felt Butch rip the wet sheet off of him. He nearly threw up from the fear.

"Come on Billllieeee, I want to seee the big bad monster in your closet! Come on, let's throw you in the closet Billy, I am sure your monster is very hungry!" He giggled manically.

He ripped Billy off his bed, disgustedly because Billy wet his pants. He threw Billy in the closet. Billy screamed as he smelled the foul air and felt the moist furry body closing in on him. He heard Butch howling with perverted evil laughter. The scream in his throat was frozen. He heard Butch push against the door, locking him inside. He felt him making the door shake with his twisted laughter. He felt Angel's breath against his neck. It was fetid and hot. Butch flung the door open and laughed in loud boozy guffaws.

"Where is your monster Billy? You fuckin little pansy!" Butch taunted. Billy ran past him and Butch laughed as he back handed him.

"Oh big scary monster, where are you? Oh I am so afraid! I am shivering and shaking with fear." he giggled with twisted delight. Billy watched in horrified fascination as Butch was pulled inside the closet. He heard the screams and crunching of bones. He almost felt sorry for Butch, but not quite.

The screams and whimpering continued for quite a while. Billy went into his mother's spare room. He called Grandma. He knew she would come and get him. He knew he would never be afraid of Butch anymore. Everyone thought Butch took off, and it was obvious that Billy's Mom was not interested in taking care of him so the courts gave custody of Billy to his grandparents. Sometimes you have to make friends with the monster to save yourself.

When Billy grew up and married, he became an excellent father and husband. When his children asked him to check the closet, he always did. His mother went to rehab, and though she never did stay sober, he made a life of his own with those who loved him. He was always grateful to his angels and especially one in particular. Sometimes angels come in disguise.